THE GRIMSTONES

MUSIC SCHOOL

by Asphyxia

the fourth magnificently
secret diary of
Martha Grimstone

ALLEN&UNWIN

SYDNEY · MELBOURNE · AUCKLAND · LONDON

Tired of your boring old cello case?

After you have displayed your musical talents, why not pack your beloved cello into a hand-knitted cello cover and display your individuality!

Designed and created by the Darksbury Knitting Guild, these covers look good while protecting your precious instrument from knocks and scrapes.

Choose from a wide range of colours, patterns and knitted structures.
A catalogue for viewing is available from the academy's administration office.

Every order placed (and paid for) this term will include a pair of gloves to match your cello cover.

Private Tuition

Need help with your musical studies?

Ensure a sound grade and sign up for one-on-one tuition in a relaxed atmosphere with an experienced, classically trained musician.

Must bring own instrument; however, upright and grand pianos are available for a small rental fee.

Contact Edith Françoise

SCHOOL RECITAL

...ay of next month

...to select a piece of music from ...e master and perform this

...is compulsory. Technical ...lomb and presentation

...ust submit their choice ...dworth for approval ... month.

Piano tuning

REASONABLE RA... AND STUDENT DISC...

contact: Ava Goo...

FOR SALE
1 x Typewriter in almost good condition (missing letter 'p')
Accompanied by 12 brand-new typewriter ribbons (9 black, 3 red)

Contact Alexander

WANTED

A ride home to Keenings Creek at the end of school term. Extra space for two trunks and a grand piano desirable.

Please speak with Amelia (First Year student)

The **Queen's** Music Academy

Music Academy

All notices MUST bear the offical Academy Stamp of Authorisation before they can be displayed on this noticeboard.

Failure to comply will result in the removal of the notice.

Surely this rule applies to this notice as well??

VERY IMPORTANT ANNOUNCEMENT

In accordance with the Education Department's Code of Practice for the Prevention and Removal of Wood-eating Pests, the academy's quarterly fumigation of ALL instruments will take place next Tuesday morning.

Students with allergies or sensitive nasal passages are advised to delay their attendance by 2 hours. Kindly inform your teacher if you will not be present for the first half of your class.

Madame Sonatine

Headmistress.

AY	WEDNESDAY	THURSDAY	FRIDAY
	harp	harp	harp
ion tion	needlepoint	aplomb	deportment
g	private lesson	composition and notation	private practic
kneory	music theory	private practice	grammar

Is your stringed instrument looking dull?

Dr J's **Orange Blossom Beeswax** is the only wax to bring a glorious sheen to your valuable instrument without becoming tacky under intense stage lights.

Try it today!

Available from Darksbury General Store.

Dr.J's **WAX** FOR STRINGED INSTRUMENTS
Beautifies and protects
all four hundred
CONTAINS ORANGE
BLOSSOM BEESWAX

FOUND

on Wednesday, near the front entrance to the assembly hall.

First published in 2013

Allen & Unwin
83 Alexander Street
Crows Nest NSW 2065
Australia
Phone: (61 2) 8425 0100
Email: info@allenandunwin.com
Web: www.allenandunwin.com

A Cataloguing-in-Publication entry is available
from the National Library of Australia
www.trove.nla.gov.au

ISBN 978 1 74331 625 2

Cover and text design by Jenine Davidson. Cover photograph by Taras Mohamed; dress and bat artwork by Asphyxia. Set in 11pt Bookman Old Style by Jenine Davidson. Internal photographs by Asphyxia, Adis Hondo (www.handinhand.com.au), Taras Mohamed (www.tarasmohamed.com), Paula Dowse and Marcel Aucar (www.marcelaucar.com.au). Artwork by Asphyxia and Jenine Davidson. Bed on p11, fish on p28 and sculptures on p39 created by Mark Downing.
This book was printed in August 2013 at Everbest Printing Co Ltd in 334 Huanshi Road South, Nansha, Guangdong, China.

1 3 5 7 9 10 8 6 4 2

Australian Government

Australia Council
for the Arts

This project has been assisted by the Australian Government through the Australia Council, its arts funding and advisory body.

THE GRIMSTONES

Created & written
by Asphyxia

Designed and typeset
by Jenine Davidson

Big Ideas, especially for story
and characters, by Paula Dowse
and Kelly Parry

Photographs by Adis Hondo,
Taras Mohamed, Marcel Aucar,
Paula Dowse and Asphyxia

Illustrations by Jenine Davidson
and Asphyxia

Fantastic editing by Elise Jones
and Eva Mills

Little ideas by Jesse Dowse

Harp advice by Saffron Zomer

Four-poster bed and Gods of
Sapientia by Mark Downing

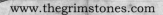

www.thegrimstones.com

SUNDAY

My Dear Diary,

Only a few more hours until we arrive at Lady Sterling's! I simply cannot wait. Please forgive my Wibbly Wobbly Writing – it can't be helped, as the wagon lurches from side to side with every pothole we cross. We borrowed our neighbour Mr Johnson's horses and they are doing their best, but I can see they are weary from pulling us all day long and will need a special feed of snargalaf pods when they finally return home.

August, who tends my family's plants and repairs our house, is escorting me to Darksbury. Before dawn broke this morning, I kissed Mama goodbye and wiped a tear from her cheek; received a firm hug from Grandpa Grimstone, who warned me not to make too much mischief; and cuddled my baby brother, Crumpet, in my arms for so long that Aunt Gertrude eventually hustled me out the door. Just as I was climbing into the wagon, she grasped me for a quick kiss. 'Attend your erudition devotedly, child,' she murmured sternly.

I still can't believe Lady Sterling has invited

me to board with her while I attend the Queen's Music Academy, on the strength of having heard me play my Epithium just once at the summer solstice party we hosted. She's the most glamorous lady I've ever known. I've only met her twice, so I'm a little nervous about how it will be. I'm secretly hoping her elegance will rub off on me, and that life in the big city will transform me somehow.

But back to our journey. At lunchtime, August brought the horses to rest at the lake by our valley's edge. We were eating cheese-and-pickle sandwiches when I felt the familiar slither of a cold breath of air against my ankle. A whirlwind! It coiled up my leg and wrapped a tentacle around my sandwich, raising goosebumps all along my arms.

My valley lives in fear of these whirlwinds – or rather, the storms that follow, for they hurtle about, ripping trees from their roots, smashing windows and tearing leaves from our most precious herbs.

Grandpa Grimstone casts spells that sometimes move the storms further away. But it leaves him so drained that I'm growing afraid for him. Surely he's too old for this. My father was onto something brilliant – he learned to manipulate the weather with intricate melodies from his Epithium. But he died before he mastered storm banishment. Now it's up to me: I must find a way to evict the storms from our valley once and for all.

I did have the idea that uncoiling a whirlwind – dispersing its impish devilishness into an ordinary breeze by turning it inside out – may fizzle out the accompanying storm. I can create a whirlwind, and have worked for months to invert the melody. Just last week I finally knew I had it! Only I couldn't test it right away, as of course the only time I ever *wanted* a whirlwind, there wasn't one to be found, anywhere.

Until today.

I was so excited that I dropped my sandwich and rushed to the back of the wagon, where the Epithium was tethered. I wriggled onto its velvet seat, my legs tangling with the ropes that held it fast, and reached for the strings. The whirlwind followed, its tickly tentacles curling around my neck and pulling at my dress. I shivered, and struck the first notes.

My music rang out through the valley, and August looked up in surprise. But I paid him no mind, for to play music that moves the weather I must channel every part of my emotions into the notes. I closed my eyes. I've practised this piece many times since last week, but never with a whirlwind coiled around my neck. I brought to mind countless storms and their damage, and just as tears welled in my eyes I felt the grip of the whirlwind weaken. My fingers rushed over the strings, and as the notes took over, the whirlwind slackened, diluted, fading into tiny particles that spilled out of the wagon, onto the ground, and drifted aimlessly away.

Triumphantly, I played the last notes.

'Miss Martha! You've your first day at school tomorrow. Don't wear yourself out now.' August smiled fondly.

'I wasn't entertaining you. August, I just dispersed my first ever whirlwind! Perhaps the storm won't follow now.' And I skippitied my feet happily in the grass.

August looked around in alarm. 'Oh flibber-guggle! I sure hope you're right about stopping

that storm – or that your music's at least delayed it, so I can make it home in time to protect your grandfather's plants. We'd best hurry along now. You pack the food. I'll hitch the horses.'

But as I gathered together the remains of our picnic, I saw the misty fragments of the whirlwind float together, amassing themselves into a cone-shaped cloud. A tentacle lifted lazily, and then another, more strongly; then suddenly the whirl-wind regained its power, coiling itself inwards and sucking upwards, drawing in grasses and leaves until it was a wild, hurtling little beast that blew itself out of sight, towards my family's home.

I sighed. Maybe my inversion melody needs a finishing touch, to ensure the whirlwind stays uncoiled. Or perhaps whirlwinds need something bigger than my unwinding tune to squash their power.

I can't help but wonder if my father's last work-sheet, written the very day of his death, holds the key. It is incomplete, but he scrawled a great many mysterious markings onto this composition – symbols I've been unable to decipher. I've worked my way steadily through his other sheets, translating enough from his cryptic notes to learn to play his melodies to bring rain, or send clouds into the distance, or settle a sunshower. But that final worksheet is another matter altogether. There is still much I don't understand. And this is why, Dear Diary, I am en route to music school. May the teachers there show me all I need to know!

MONDAY

We arrived at Lady Sterling's last night just as a party ended. Guests were streaming out the door, and Mr Johnson's wagon seemed frightfully shabby in the driveway next to all the elegant carriages being hitched for the road. The guests were dressed in furs and fabrics that would make Mama swoon. Lady Sterling herself was the grandest of all, with delicate jewels at her throat and wrist. She wore the very dress Mama and I made for her, its long folds shimmering softly around her ankles.

August made a quick bow. 'Ma'am, I must make haste, to get the Epithium to the school and return home this very night. A storm is coming.' He ruffled my hair, and I flung myself at him, squeezing my arms hard around his waist; then he re-hitched Mr Johnson's horses and was gone.

Lady Sterling took me into her arms. 'Martha, my dear! I'm so thrilled you're here at last. You must be so weary.'

She led me through the house, past servants carrying wood for the fire and trays of desserts, and lingering guests bidding one another farewell, into – you won't believe this! – my very own wing. Yes, I've an <u>ENTIRE WING</u> of the house for myself. There's a sitting room with a daybed, an occasional table and shelves full of enticing books, and an indoor bathroom with gold pipes to carry the water away. Most magnificent of all is the bed, with its enormous four posters and drapes of gold and green. Above me, on the railings, carvings of fish and oyster shells dance. Last night it was like sleeping under the sea – as if I were some water nymph or ocean goddess.

Lady Sterling grasped the arm of a passing servant, a pretty girl in a demure black dress. 'Martha dear, meet Rose. If you need anything at all, please ask her.'

Rose has a sweet face, and her cheeks are like delicate pink petals. Her lips moved but I didn't hear the slightest sound.

'Pardon?' I asked politely.

'Would you like a glass of milk?' Rose whispered.

Before I could answer, Lady Sterling leaned between us. 'Dear child, I'm afraid I must hurry away, as I've guests to pay my respects to, but I shall see you first thing in the morning and take you to school.' With that, she swept from the room.

'Yes, please!' I told Rose. Then I was alone, and so terribly excited I felt sure I couldn't possibly sleep. The bed was so high I could barely clamber onto it, but luckily I've been training in case I ever run away to join the circus, so I did my best flip and landed right in the middle of a silky, feathery pile of eiderdowns. (This morning I noticed a foot stool had been thoughtfully placed beside the bed, for the less acrobatic of Lady Sterling's guests.)

Just as I'd settled into the bed like a princess, Rose returned with some milk and a biscuit on a tray. We smiled at each other shyly and she set the tray on my lap. Then she tucked the covers around me and slipped out of the room, all without saying a word.

The whirlwind music and all that travel must have exhausted me, or maybe the milk calmed me, for I fell into a deep, watery sleep.

I was woken by the tinkling of a small glass bell. Lady Sterling stood in the doorway, fresh in a sophisticated green suit with a cascading bustle.

'Thank the heavens! I thought you'd never wake; Rose was unable to rouse you. Welcome to Darksbury, my dear. Now if you'll forgive the rush, we must hurry. Have you a warm coat?'

The streets between Lady Sterling's resplendent manor and the Queen's Music Academy were full of horses and carriages and people shouting, and men carrying boxes into the fine shops that lined the roads. People stepped out of the shops holding boxes wrapped with bows, almost bumping into the delivery men, and a horse splashed mud from a puddle all over an elegant young lady, causing the man she was with to shriek in horror. It was both frightening and exciting after the quiet streets of Gloomington, my tiny village.

We reached a high wall with a narrow archway cut into it. People streamed into the archway, and more people elbowed their way back out again. Lady Sterling took hold of both my shoulders. 'You will make me proud, Martha, I know it. Now, I must dash to my meeting, but I'll be home in time for supper, and you will tell me every single thing about your day, yes? Now go on, and good luck.' She kissed the top of my head and was gone.

I paused, waiting for a break in the crowd. Around my neck hung a small vial from Grandpa Grimstone. It contains the essence of home, he told me. I closed my fingers over it, then pushed into the throng.

Inside the archway I found myself staring up at the most magnificent, ancient building I'd ever seen.

A shrill bell rang out across the grounds, and from the balcony a man with a megaphone shouted for us all to enter the ballroom. It didn't matter that I'd no idea where it was, for I was carried along with the tide of students, bumping into violin and flute cases, pressed against long ringlets and tailored woollen blazers. Everyone talked at once.

How were your holidays?

Did you find...

...performed at the royal...

...practising endlessly, but...

There you are!

Wait till I show you...

The ballroom walls were lined with embossed green paper, and sparkling chandeliers lit the way to a large raised stage draped with red velvet curtains. We were pressed into rows of metal folding chairs, and I found myself sitting beside a thin, pale-faced boy with big ears, who was tap-tappitying his feet on the floor and strumming his fingers against the chair leg, humming a tune that sounded a little like the bread-bird song I once composed. I peered at him in surprise, for I had never in my life come across another child who cannot help themself from making music at every turn.

I leaned towards him.

'Hi. I'm Martha Grimstone.'

He held out his hand. 'Albert.' His fingers were cold but his smile was crooked and friendly. 'I play the harp. It's my second year here. What do you—'

But just then a hush fell over the crowd as a tall, polished-looking lady stepped onto the stage, separated from us by a gaping hole that I later saw was the orchestra pit. She peered at us through theatre glasses.

'That's Madame Sonatine, the headmistress,' Albert whispered.

'Welcome, pupils, to a new term at the Queen's Music Academy,' Madame Sonatine declared. 'As you know, famous musicians made their beginnings here. Our fine halls are lined with their portraits – Menacino Hugastli, who is playing for the Royal Family this very day; the highly distinguished Piola de Grue; and our brilliant Phelius Blackwell, who just last week thanked me yet again for his tuition at the school. It is due to his musical education here that he is renowned worldwide.

'Pupils! I expect you all to become distinguished and talented: to do this school proud. Then we shall see *your* portraits upon these walls! Study hard, my dears, study hard!'

Someone in the audience gave a small gurgling laugh, and it reminded me so of Crumpet. He's the sweetest child who ever existed! A terrible wave of homesickness swept over me, even though I'd only kissed him goodbye a day ago.

Polite applause broke out amongst the students and we were dismissed. Albert led me to a noticeboard outside in the hallway. All the classes and students were listed, and it seemed we had to determine our timetables from this. Albert wrote his on his arm, and I scribbled mine onto a piece of paper while bumping elbows with about a hundred other students.

My timetable:

MONDAY	TUESDAY	WEDNESDAY	THURSDAY	FRIDAY
harp	harp	harp	harp	harp
Latin	composition and notation	needlepoint	aplomb	deportment
music theory	drawing	private lesson	composition and notation	private practice
harmony	music theory	music theory	private practice	grammar

I gave a little skip of excitement. I can start every day with my beloved Epithium! Several other subjects intrigue me, too: Why would a music school teach drawing? I declare composition and notation shall be my favourite! I will compose piece after piece, until I can stop a storm in its tracks! (Which reminds me, I hope August made it back in time. Did my music delay the storm at all?) And I'll learn to notate my compositions correctly, in much clearer form than my father did. Even more excitingly, I shall learn the meanings of all those symbols he scrawled on his final worksheet. I will be the most dedicated student in the whole school!

Disappointingly, I'll still have to study Latin, grammar and deportment. Aunt Gertrude has been drilling the finer points of these monotonous subjects into me for years, making me balance books on my head as she holds a ruler to my back to check I am sufficiently ladylike. Dear Diary, I was hoping I would be freed from these trivialities, and allowed to play the Epithium all day long.

Albert and I joined a small group of students heading up some stairs to harp class. Then we turned down a narrow, dark corridor, threaded through another, and descended some steep, rickety steps that led down, down into darkness. I paused to look back, trying to memorise the way, and in that instant the other students disappeared.

I ducked through the only door I could see and discovered a library – a large space filled with leather-bound books, many ragged at the spine.

I ran towards the far side of the room, hoping to catch the other students beyond the door. A thin, stooped man with round gold eyeglasses glowered at me. 'Quiet please, ladies,' he called, even though there was only me.

I forced myself to slow to a hurried walk, willing my feet not to **THUMP-THUMP** so loudly on the wooden floor, but once through the door, in yet another corridor indistinguishable from all the others, and seeing no sign of Albert, I broke into a run.

I ran for what seemed like forever, glared down upon by portraits of historic musicians, the walls creaking and windows rattling as I passed. I wished I had Crumpet in my arms – he'd puff some magical air, say a sweet word to calm my heart, and point me in the right direction. That's the handy thing about having a baby brother with the gift of magic. But then muffled piano notes floated towards me, and I followed them to a wooden door.

Stepping inside, at last I found the students I'd lost gathered around various instruments. There was a grand piano, two regular pianos, and a few harpsichords. And right there next to the grand piano stood my cherished Epithium, safely delivered by August, its strings glowing, the red velvet seat calling me. I rushed over and laid my cheek against its cool, dark wood. Calm settled over me, and my world righted itself.

'Martha, I thought we'd lost you!' Albert said.

The door opened and an enormous figure emerged... Mr Bloodworth, my harp teacher.

Mr Bloodworth by M. Grimstone ⤷

He strode to the front of the room, and when he spoke his voice boomed as though we were in an auditorium instead of a space the size of my dining room at home, with only six students before him.

'Good morning, my pupils of harp and piano. Let's see if you've improved over the break.' He pointed to a boy sitting at the grand piano. 'Friederich Ealdwine, this is your final year. Did you successfully master Sternberg's *Nocturna de Muse* during the holiday?'

Friederich, wearing a stiff dark suit, his blond hair neatly combed, said: 'I did, sir. I look forward to playing it for you.' His voice was confident, with a commanding Dirgeton accent.

Mr Bloodworth's eyes roamed, and settled upon me. 'I see we have a new student amongst us.'

He stroked his eyebrows, twirling the left one into a little ringlet. 'Well? Come on, girl, introduce yourself.'

I stood, holding onto the Epithium for support. His bloodshot eyes bored into me. 'I'm Martha Grimstone, sir.' I paused, and when he didn't respond, I continued, 'This is my Epithium, which my father invent—'

'Yes, yes, I don't need your life's history. Let's get on with it. Pair up. Piano: scales. Harp: arpeggios. Go!'

I gulped, not sure what he was asking us to do, but a girl tapped me on the shoulder and whispered, 'Be my partner?'

I nodded, turning to face her. She had a wide, friendly face and clear blue eyes. She reminded me

of a doll I used to play with when I was small, until I dropped her in the creek and ruined her.

'I play scales on the piano, you play arpeggios on your…on that *thing*…and we have to get the timing together, okay?'

She seated herself at a piano, with such elegant posture that I was glad Aunt Gertrude wasn't here to compare her to me. I wheeled my Epithium over, parked it beside her, and settled on the seat.

'You start,' I suggested.

Just as the girl's notes rang through the room, so too did those of two other pianos and harps. Mr Bloodworth clapped his hands over his ears.

'SILENCE!' He bellowed. He turned to the mantelpiece and set a metronome. A steady *tick, tick, tick* beat through the room. 'YOU, eight bars,' he said, gesturing to me and the doll-girl, 'then YOU, then YOU, and back to the start. COMMENCE.'

The doll-girl's scales rang out, melodious and clear. Half a second behind her, I struggled to fit my arpeggios to her notes, but before I could make it work our eight bars were over. The class went around and around, and each time my fingers trembled nervously and my notes came out wrong.

After arpeggios, we practised chords. Mr Blood-worth charged in on something Albert was doing wrong, and the doll-girl leaned over to whisper in my ear: 'My name's Viola Verlene.'

'But you play the piano!' I protested. Then I clapped my hand over my mouth, because surely that was rude.

She smiled, a broad, open smile full of warmth. 'It's all right. My parents named me that because they needed a viola player in the family. It is of great disappointment to them that I can merely play the piano. I expect they'll forgive me some day.'

'Why did they need a viola player?'

'My family have always been musicians. We play for royal families and international festivals. My aunt, a viola player, died not long before I was born. Sadly, we are still short. And even my piano skills aren't quite up to par, which is why I'm here instead of performing with them in Tylesberg right now.'

Mr Bloodworth shouted for silence. 'Your goal for this class is to master Melancholski's Somberto in E Minor. A complicated piece indeed, essential for any true musician. The whole school will play it together at the end-of-term benefit concert.' He handed us each a folder of sheet music, filled with pages of elaborate notes.

I raised my hand. 'Sir? I've another goal, also. I wish to permanently uncoil a whirlwind, or learn how to stomp—'

'Did I ask if you had any other goals? No, I did not! In this class, *I* set your goals. Now, we'll begin with the first page.'

I bit my lip and turned to the music he'd given us. I played the first note, and then the second, and the third, but my fingers were pushed into foreign shapes and it felt awkward, clumsy.

And that, Dear Diary, is all I can possibly tell you about my day, for my eyes are closing. I even used the footstool to climb into bed tonight. The fish dance above me, and I'm sure to dream of mermaids and sea creatures. If only I had Crumpet here – this bed feels frightfully big without Mama on one side of me and Crumpet on the other.

Goodnight, dear book.

TUESDAY

I was wrong! Drawing is going to be my very favourite class. Miss Fairclough is our teacher, and she is so sweet I can actually see her heart beating through her blouse. She wears a blue sailor dress and has long coiled plaits.

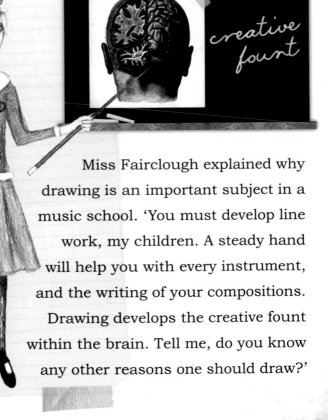

creative fount

Miss Fairclough explained why drawing is an important subject in a music school. 'You must develop line work, my children. A steady hand will help you with every instrument, and the writing of your compositions. Drawing develops the creative fount within the brain. Tell me, do you know any other reasons one should draw?'

Viola Verlene raised her hand. 'Ma'am, my family creates programmes, posters and handbills for our performances. My uncle draws superbly, and his illustrations always attract the biggest crowds.'

'There you go. Drawing is an essential skill for any working musician. You are to keep slips of paper with you at all times, and make sketches at every opportunity. Show me your work each week, and I shall critique it. Please try especially to draw people, for attractive people on a poster will always pull a crowd. Now, let me show you how to crosshatch. Take out your pencils, please.'

Do you know what crosshatching is? It's scribbling! You scribble this way and that, more in some places than others, and what do you know, after a while the drawing looks rich and alive. I had no idea real drawing could be this easy! Aunt Gertrude always tells me off for scribbling while she educates me, and now I can tell her it's the makings of fine art. Today I drew Mr Bloodworth and taped it in several pages back, so now you'll know what he looks like.

I'm writing all out of order, though. Before

drawing, we had composition and notation. Our teacher, Mr Blanche, has a shock of white hair and bright-red eyes.

'He's albino,' Albert whispered.

'Good morning, class,' Mr Blanche intoned. 'Today we shall examine the compositions of Piola de Grue and Shadov Macabriov, to understand their brilliance.'

My mouth dropped open, for this had not been my understanding of the class. I raised my hand as high as I possibly could.

Mr Blanche trained his scarlet eyes on me. 'Oh! The new girl. Yes, what is it?'

'Excuse me, sir, but when will we begin composing our own music?'

He raised his eyebrows so high they almost left his forehead. 'Your own music? I shouldn't think so.'

'But it's a composition class! Surely we will compose?'

He laughed. Albert poked me in my side and subtly shook his head, so I knew I'd asked entirely the wrong question. But Grandpa Grimstone says an enquiring mind is the mark of high intelligence!

Mr Blanche rolled his eyes. 'We have an impertinent one! Child, you presume your compositions to be worthy of notation? I think not! The purpose of this class is to discover the brilliance of our ancestors. We do not encourage students to pen their trite little ditties.'

I glared at him. 'I do *not* compose trite little ditties. I invent music that brings rain when plants are thirsty, and turns it to sunshine when we need warmth and joy. I just need to compose the right music to banish—'

'Girl, what you invent are tall tales. Of course music does not bring changes to the weather.'

'It does! I can show you! Look!' And I made to run and fetch my Epithium.

But Mr Blanche stood in the doorway with his arms crossed, barring my exit. 'Sit down, child. Now, does anyone know what year Piola de Grue composed her Epiquity for Viola?'

I stomped back to my seat. Mr Blanche is wrong! I do *not* invent tall tales! And if he's an expert on the great compositions of our ancestors, he should know about music's true power.

So as you can see, composition and notation is not going to be one of my favourite subjects after all.

SATURDAY

Dear Diary,

Who knew the Queen's Music Academy could tire me out so? Each day I've applied myself to drills set by Mr Bloodworth, made little sketches for Miss Fairclough, tried my best not to yawn through needlepoint, aplomb, deportment or grammar, and dragged myself home to Lady Sterling's, where we eat by the fire in the parlour. Except on Wednesday night, when she hosted a benefit: I was so tired my face almost fell into my supper of pickled seahorse mousse topped with tickleberries, so I excused myself and retired to my very own wing.

Every night I fall (well, flip) into bed, drink Rose's milk, and sleep in a world of black oceans and dancing fish until Lady Sterling wakes me with her bell. It seems Rose is just too quiet to wake me, and I am perpetually running late for school.

Today it's the weekend, and I woke at almost midday to find the house perfectly quiet. No Lady Sterling in sight, nor Rose, nor a single maid nor butler. Large bell-shaped flowers bloomed outside my window, which put me in mind to pick some for Lady Sterling as a thank you for all she's done for me. But when I got to the garden I was completely distracted by an enchanting cottage with wide double doors, one of them open to the pond. I crept towards it and peered inside.

'Martha! You're awake at last!'

Lady Sterling sat within. Gone were her splendid clothes and jewels. Her shirt was streaked with clay, and her hair was pinned back messily. Before her stood a sculpture, with crudely cut sockets for eyes and jutting cheekbones. The cottage was a workshop, its walls hung with sculpting tools, and there were sacks of sand and bags of clay piled inside the door. Lady Sterling poked a lump of clay onto the cheek and smoothed it with her thumb. I stared in astonishment.

'Come on in, dear. I'll just finish Tempesta's face.'

'That's Tempesta? The ancient goddess of wild weather and storms?' Aunt Gertrude made me study the traditional deities. 'She's beautiful.'

'She is, isn't she? I thought I'd give her a whirlwind for hair. A little uncustomary, I know.'

'But very fitting. What will you do with her when she's done?'

'I'll have Edgar, the garden boy, build an arbour for her, surrounding her with twisting vines to represent the wind.'

With a wooden spatula, Lady Sterling smoothed

a roll of clay she'd placed under the nose. I watched as she transformed it into a pair of rounded lips. Then she wiped her hands on her trousers and covered Tempesta with a damp cloth. 'Let's take a stroll in the garden before lunch. We'll have to make that ourselves, I'm afraid, as I've given all the staff a day off. It's the only way to get a moment's peace around here.'

She linked her arm through mine and we set off down a charming path lined with hedgerows and wildflowers. Amongst them grew something I recognised – tiny ficklepod seedlings! Lady Sterling had germinated the seeds Grandpa Grimstone gave her.

'Tell me, Martha, after a week at the Queen's Music Academy, do you feel it's all you'd hoped for?'

I didn't know what to say. The Queen's Musical Academy is NOT all I've hoped for at all… but how could I tell Lady Sterling that, when she's been so generous?

I chose my words carefully. 'It's clearly been the starting point for many fine musicians. But I wonder how long it will be before I'm taught what I need to know.'

'And what is it you need to know?'

'How to save my valley from storms, of course!'

Lady Sterling squeezed my arm. 'Well, I don't expect they have a subject devoted just to that. But garner all you can from your studies, Martha, and perhaps eventually it will become clear. I'm sure it takes a tremendous amount of patience to become the kind of musician who can move the heavens.'

We stopped before a pair of enormous stone statues. Lady Sterling brushed a cobweb from one of the goat-heads. 'These are the twin Gods of Sapientia, the guardians of knowledge and wisdom. They founded the very first schools, to enable children to learn.'

'Did you sculpt these, too?'

'I did.'

'But they're enormous! How did you carry them down here?'

Lady Sterling laughed. 'I cut them into pieces while the clay was still wet, and once they'd been fired in my kiln, Edgar reassembled them for me here. I sculpt, he builds.'

She gestured grandly to the statues. 'Now, Martha, may the gods grant you the patience you need to learn your craft.'

So, there. I am resolved! I shall simply be patient, and eventually I shall learn what I came for. (Probably not from Mr Blanche. Still, I shall try to pay attention, for who knows, perhaps one of the great masters we study will have just the techniques I need.)

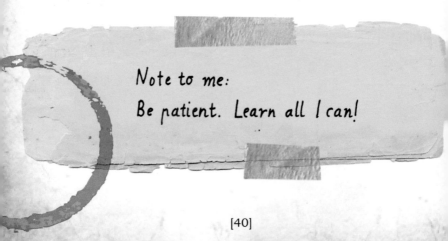

Note to me:
Be patient. Learn all I can!

We returned to the house, and while Lady Sterling refreshed herself I set about making lunch. The only food I know how to prepare is cheese-and-pickle sandwiches, but there wasn't a single pickle in Lady Sterling's kitchen, nor a loaf of bread, so I improvised:

I carried the tray into the parlour and lit the fire. We'd just started lunch when a great cloud of smoke billowed from the fireplace. Lady Sterling fanned the fire vigorously with a newspaper, but that only made it worse. 'The chimney must be blocked,' she exclaimed. 'I'll call for the sweep on Monday. We need water to put this out.' And she was gone.

Sputtering, I peered up the chimney...and saw the fluttering of wings. Bats! They've taken up residence there, of all places.

'Sorry, little ones,' I called. 'I hope we didn't burn you.'

In answer, a tiny bat plopped down and landed square on my cheek. I lifted it into my palm and stroked its soft, furry body. 'We'll find you a new home, I promise. This isn't the best place for a family.' It flapped its wings and disappeared back up the chimney.

Just then, the doorbell rang. When Lady Sterling didn't answer it, I dashed through the foyer and flung open the door. Before me stood two rotund men with long, curly moustaches.

'Montgomery B. Brownelowe Esquire's Antique Reassembly Co. at your service, mademoiselle. Where would you like us to place your delivery?'

They bowed towards an enormous wooden crate. Flummoxed, I cast around for the correct answer. 'Here, in the foyer?'

They unrolled a small square of red carpet and, grunting loudly, carried the crate inside and placed it carefully on top.

At that same moment, Lady Sterling reappeared. 'Oh! Is this the grandfather clock?'

The men bowed. 'We offer our condolences for your recent bereavement.'

Bereavement? I gasped. But Lady Sterling smiled graciously. 'His passing was not unexpected. Let's have it in the parlour.' To me, she said, 'My great-uncle. He was very old. He always promised he'd leave me his clock.'

If the Montgomery B.s were annoyed with me for giving them the wrong instructions, they didn't show it. An hour later, the clock pendulum swung from side to side with a resounding *tock, tock, tock,* and I admired

the intricate carvings rising from the wood panels: little bats, sitting on ornate curlicues sprouting tiny embossed herbs and flowers. I recognised miniature mahogany thornbells, like those in our garden at home by the crypt. Beautiful!

At last we went back to our lunch – but just as Lady Sterling was taking a bite, an enormous BOOM, BOOM, BOOM chimed through the house.

'GOODNESS!' Lady Sterling shrieked, leaping into the air and knocking the tray of food so that our lunch exploded everywhere.

I put my hand over my mouth in horror, but moments later she was laughing as she picked bits of cake out of my hair.

'That clock is much, much louder than I remembered it,' she said. 'I do hope I haven't made a mistake.'

WEDNESDAY

I'm doing as Lady Sterling suggests: learning all I can from the Queen's Music Academy, and applying it as best I can to my own music.

So, now that Mr Blanche has shown us a good many compositions from renowned musicians, I'm starting to see how one writes them down and have set myself the task of recording my whirlwind inversion music. I know the whirlwind just re-coils itself afterwards, but perhaps once the music is written on paper one of my teachers will tell me how to fix it.

This morning before harp class started I was working on my whirlwind composition when Mr Bloodworth appeared.

'Good morning, class!' he shouted, and I res-isted the impulse to plug my ears with my fingers. Instead, I hastily poked my worksheet into my case and sat up tall, at attention.

'The time has come. You are not ready. Not worthy. Regardless, today we practise Melancholski's somberto. You first.' He pointed a thick finger at Albert and gestured that Viola Verlene should accompany him on the piano.

I closed my eyes in anticipation. It's one thing to pore over notes on the page, to try to work out how to play them – but you can't understand the true power of any music until you hear it played properly.

The notes sounded through the room, hesitantly at first, then more confidently as Albert and Viola found their place with one another. The melody was lovely, full of fast trills and harmonies that grew to a pleasing crescendo…but nothing *happened.* I'd imagined a piece this complicated would hold power – immense, magical power!

As Albert and Viola played their final notes, Mr Bloodworth nodded. 'A good start. Albert, on the second page, third bar, your notes were off. Work on that. Viola, you were behind Albert through the third section. Faster, child! Synchronise!'

Then it was my turn, and I had to keep up with Friederich. I have been practising – really I have! But I felt flummoxed, and the whole piece came out utterly distorted.

On the second page, Mr Bloodworth shouted, 'SILENCE! Friederich, play alone. Disgraceful, girl! Is the problem you, or is it that excuse for an instrument you play on?'

Aghast, I couldn't bring myself to reply. If only I could play *my* music. Or any music at all that the Epithium is meant to play; then my fingers are filled with knowing. But since I arrived I haven't been able to play a single note of my own choosing.

Later, in my private lesson, Mr Bloodworth sat by the window, eyes on the sky while I battled with the somberto's trills.

'Too slow,' he roared after my first run. 'It seems it's YOU, not your instrument.'

On my second run, he interrupted me partway through. 'You used that pedal in a different place last time.'

I stared at him, uncomprehending.

'The somberto is written as if for piano. To translate it to the harp, you need to plan precisely where to press a pedal, and which pedal it will be. Until you have annotated your sheet music, you will make no progress.'

I nodded. 'Yes, sir.' There was silence, and finally I asked, 'Err, what is the correct way to … annotate?'

Mr Bloodworth resumed his gaze out the window. 'Your notation teacher will cover that.' Then, impatiently, clicking his tongue, he grabbed my music sheet. Pulling a pencil from his shirt pocket, he quickly showed me a few marks. 'See, here, this pedal – note it like that. Do the entire piece before your next class.'

'Yes, sir.'

I paused, waiting for instruction. Was I supposed to play again, or was the lesson over now that we'd identified this task? Mr Bloodworth remained silent.

'Sir?' I asked tentatively. When there was no response, I pressed on. 'I wondered if you'd take a look at my whirlwind inversion composition?' I held forth the music I had created.

Mr Bloodworth sighed heavily. 'Your request is premature, miss. I've no interest in homemade compositions until you master the basics. Let's hear your trills again, faster now.'

I gritted my teeth hard then, so I wouldn't cry. I focused on the sheet music and settled my fingers into the trills. They did come out a little faster this time, and even to me they sounded marginally better. I played them three times through without stopping, because I didn't want to look at Mr Bloodworth again.

Suddenly something flashed through my mind. The notation Mr Bloodworth had shown me. I'd seen it before. Yes! On my father's last worksheet!

'STOP!' Mr Bloodworth bellowed, and I leapt in fright.

'Just when you were improving, your trills fire everywhere!'

'I'm sorry, sir.'

'You need to practise, girl, *practise*. I'll leave you

to it. Don't forget to annotate.' And Mr Bloodworth strode from the room, banging the door behind him.

As soon as he'd gone I rummaged through my case. Even though I hadn't had a moment to look at it since I arrived, I've kept my father's last worksheet close, always. I pulled it out and studied it carefully. So *that's* what he meant by those squiggles. This would give the whole melody an entirely different flavour. A horde of other markings are still foreign to me, but it's a start, Dear Diary.

IT'S A START!

FRIDAY

Oh! I was just settling down to sleep when there was a quiet tapping at the window. My bird was silhouetted against the moon, an envelope in its beak! In my valley this bird follows me everywhere, but this is the first time I've seen it in the city. It perches on my shoulder now as I open the letter, written in Mama's handwriting.

from the sewing table
of Velvetta Grimstone

Dearest Martha,

How quiet the house seems since your departure. We think of you daily and hope you are learning musical brilliance from all those distinguished teachers. How do you fare boarding with Lady Sterling? Grandpa Grimstone expresses a concern that you may be causing havoc, but I assured him you seem quite mature now.

Crumpet does keep me extraordinarily busy!

Martha, I've a new appreciation for all you did with him. Each morning I take him outdoors, else he is quite unbearable for the day. August has him next, and they complete the garden chores together. Then Crumpet studies magic with Grandpa Grimstone for several hours. In the afternoon he is content to be with me as I work. He loves to scramble onto my shelves, sweep everything off, and then call out little magical words to stop the items in midair, orchestrating them in a glorious symphony. Needless to say, my sewing workshop is now highly organised. Gertrude is no longer fit to behead me.

Now that she is not spending her time educating you, Gertrude has the house polished to within an inch of its life and is stocking the pantry at an alarming rate. At least we can be certain not to starve once winter is upon us. I hear her and August whispering, but I've no idea what they are planning. When August goes on your behalf to fetch the milk, Gertrude goes with him, her arm in his. It is marvellous to see young love blossoming. It reminds me of my time with Mortimer.

A dreadful storm blew in just after you left. August tells us you tried to disperse its whirlwind, but perhaps you only angered it, for it was the worst storm we've had in some time. I do hope your teachers can refine your technique. The kitchen window was smashed by the toppling of the huge mortemberry tree. Poor Gertrude has been working in darkness since it was boarded up. As soon as I've finished this dress for Estella Fife, I'll turn over my coins so August can buy new glass.

Grandpa Grimstone continues his work on potions to cast away the storms, but frankly I feel his interest is waning. We are waiting for you now, Martha, to do something wondrous with your music. I do believe dear Mortimer was on the right track.

I must go now, sweetheart, for it's time to put Crumpet to bed. I admit to a few evenings when I've been too absorbed in my sewing to settle him down in time, and that was a disaster, as I'm sure you will know. I am learning.

All my love, Mama

PS, I confess I do miss you terribly! Especially in bed at night, as Crumpet is far more wriggly to cuddle than you are.

NO! I made the storm *worse*? I don't see how I will EVER cure our valley of storms! Mr Bloodworth doesn't think I'm worthy of such a thing because my trills are too slow, and Mr Blanche has no idea music can nudge your heart, much less orchestrate the weather! I miss my home and my family most dreadfully – especially thinking of them all suffering through that storm in the parlour, and me not even there with them.

I shall open the vial Grandpa Grimstone gave me.

essence of home

Well, now I feel even more homesick, because the scent of home is all around me, dusty, sour and familiar. But one of the bats from the chimney has flown in and nestled on my other shoulder, which is very comforting, even if it is leaving a shadow of soot on my nightgown.

It appears my bird is waiting for a reply.

 from M Grimstone's private wing

Dear Mama and Grandpa Grimstone,
Aunt Gertrude, August and Crumpet,
I'm so sorry I couldn't send the storm away.
I tried!

It's frightfully grand at Lady Sterling's, and my bed is like a cloud. Grandpa Grimstone, I haven't caused any trouble AT ALL.

Lady Sterling tells me to study hard, and I'm doing my best, though so far it seems my teachers do not know much about storm management — or, if they do, are yet to share it with me. Never fear, I am practising being Lady of Pertinacious Perseverence (that one's for you,

Aunt Gertrude) and will keep trying.

Crumpet, I do so wish you were here! I need you to explain to Lady Sterling's bats that they simply must move out of the chimney, as we are freezing without a fire in the parlour. Her chimney sweep refuses to tend to the chimney until they've vacated. He is very fond of bats. I feel them trying to communicate with me, but I don't understand them the way you would. Also, I'm sure you could tell Lady Sterling's grandfather clock to chime more quietly. It won't listen to me.

Much love to you all and many big kisses upon Crumpet especially.

Martha Grimstone   X X X

Now everything feels a bit more right, and I am reminded I must persist! I really must. My valley depends on me. So I shall close my eyes and try again to sleep, with the bat nuzzled against my neck.

MONDAY

Dear Diary,

How the weeks fly. I spend every spare moment working on my whirlwind inversion composition. I've used all I've learned to write the notes correctly: neatly organised into bars and stanzas. But for the essential part that made the whirlwind disperse, I channelled sadness, anger and frustration into my playing – and of course I've no way to write this.

Today we were in the school dining room for our noonday meal, Albert and I strumming a nice little rhythm together on the table with our forks, when Madame Sonatine interrupted us.

'Pupils! Pupils! An announcement. I trust you have been studying hard and striving for excellence with every note. As did Sternberg himself, when he studied here in these very halls! Now, on the first day of next month we shall hold a small recital.

THE Queen's Music Academy

SCHOOL RECITAL

First day of next month

select a piece of music from

Each of you is to prepare a piece of your own choosing, from your favourite master. You will be assessed not only on your technical accuracy, but on aplomb and presentation, too.'

You know exactly what I was thinking, don't you, Diary? At last, I'll have the chance to prove that my music *can* move the weather! In fact, I shall orchestrate an entire year's worth of seasons – a demonstration of every single thing I know how to do! I realise I'm not an old master...*yet*...but someday I will surely be:

Lady Martha of Magnificent Music.

HOORAY!

I was so excited that the little rhythm I'd been making with Albert bubbled up into a song – my very favourite waterweed song from home, *tra-la-la*-ing its way out of my throat in great happy swirls – and there was no way I could possibly have stopped it!

Only it stopped all of its own accord when I

realised that everyone was staring at me. Albert's eyes were goggling, and Madame Sonatine's face was cold indeed.

'Sorry,' I sputtered.

Albert regained some composure and winked at me. But Madame Sonatine glared. 'Out, Miss Grimstone! Express your excitement elsewhere in the school.'

'Y…yes, ma'am.' I fled the room, everybody still staring. Two small teardrops streaked down my cheeks.

I'd show them! I'd go straight to my Epithium, and begin composing my *Meteorological Showcase*.

I set off for the music room at a run, but suddenly I wasn't where I'd thought I was. Was I lost? After all this time spent walking these halls? The walls were papered with a pattern I'd not seen before. I saw a door set with the same pattern, oddly small, and I pushed it open.

Peculiarly, I found myself onstage in the ball-room. I stepped forward, into what could have been a spotlight had the stage been lit. I imagined myself here with my Epithium, and made a small curtsey to a crowd of invisible spectators. We'd be assessed on aplomb as well as musicality, Madame Sonatine had said.

Have I told you about aplomb? It's important here – there's a whole subject devoted to it, taught by Madame Sonatine herself. Aplomb is how you stand on a stage. It's about looking poised and magnificent, and pretending you don't have fire-flies swarming in your stomach and tiny drums pounding in your chest. We practise by standing on an imaginary stage and looking the audience (our classmates) in the eye. Every part of me always wants to look away. My fingers fidget, and my toes rock me from side to side. 'Stand *still*, Miss Grimstone,' Madame Sonatine cries, throwing up her gloved hands in despair.

When we've finished playing a piece, if someone compliments us or we hear applause, we are to bow our head graciously as though it were our due, even if we've done the most appalling job. We're to save the tears for once we've left the stage. Madame Sonatine has us imagine dreadful scenarios, such as discovering we have walked onstage with the incorrect instrument, or falling off the stage altogether, and we must practise handling all disasters with aplomb. But she hasn't covered what to do when one inadvertently bursts into song in the dining hall during announcements.

I climbed down into the orchestra pit and trailed my fingers along the wall, my nails scraping the paint with a satisfying screech. And a little *plink*.

A PLINK?

I ran my fingers over that part of the wall again. Yes, a PLINK. I realised it hid a door – no handle, just a door. I gave it a push and it creaked open.

Wonky stone stairs led down into murky – irresistible – shadows, and I followed. The walls were of unpainted stone, and I found myself in a dim corridor illuminated by a speck of light from somewhere ahead. The corridor was peppered with doors, and each opened into a small, windowless cell. What purpose have these rooms in a music school? Were they used in times past to banish naughty or inadequate students, such as myself, until we promised to be good? I shuddered.

I followed the light, and you simply won't believe what I found. A candle burned within a chamber, and beside it, in the corner, huddled Viola Verlene! Her eyes were red.

'Viola? What's wrong?' I rushed to her.

She attempted a smile. 'You found my hiding spot.'

'You come here all the time?'

'I do,' she confessed. 'It's my best place in the school, apart from the turret.'

'I've been looking for the turret!' I cried. 'But I don't know the way.'

'I'll show you. But that's where I go when I'm happy. I have to wait until these tears have dried.'

'What's wrong?'

Viola sighed, extracted a handkerchief from her pinafore pocket, and dabbed at her nose. 'I just miss my brother.'

'But you'll see him at the end of term, yes?'

'I'll never see him again! He's dead. And he was my best friend.'

Poor Viola! I settled beside her, our shoulders touching, the stone cool against my back. If something were to happen to my beloved Crumpet I would *never* walk or speak again!

'You must miss him dreadfully,' I said quietly.

'I do. He made me laugh all the time. Whenever my parents were angry, or strict, he'd make faces behind them until I giggled. And he'd impersonate the important people we performed for, without their realising, until my sides nearly split from holding in the laughter. He was a musical genius, too, Martha. It's because of him my family has been so successful. With his violin, it didn't matter that my piano was only average. But now everyone expects me to shine, and it's too much. I'll never have his brilliance. *Never*.'

Tears spurted from Viola's eyes like tiny diamonds, hitting the wall with a melodious tinkle before splattering us both until we were sodden.

Finally, the tears stopped. Viola sniffled, wiping her eyes with her sleeve. 'Come on, let's go to the turret to dry off. It's always windy up there. Maybe it will cheer me up.'

Viola held out her candle and led us through a maze of damp cells and up a narrow, spiral staircase that opened abruptly into a small round room – the turret: ⟶

Viola smiled, and I couldn't help but smile back. I told her about the recital. 'The piece we choose is to be from one of the old masters – but I'm going to play my own composition!'

Viola gasped. 'Will it move the weather? Truly?'

I nodded. 'I shall prepare the finest display of rain, sunshine and wind for us all to enjoy.'

She smiled radiantly. 'In that case, I shall sing as I play. It's a marvellous way to distract people from the mediocrity of my skill.'

'You sing, too?' I asked, thrilled.

She nodded. 'I love to sing. But my parents won't break convention and allow me to sing during our performances. The teachers here agree that it's simply not done. When I'm alone I always sing as I play and it sounds wonderful! If you can play your own composition, then I shall make up my very own rules, too!'

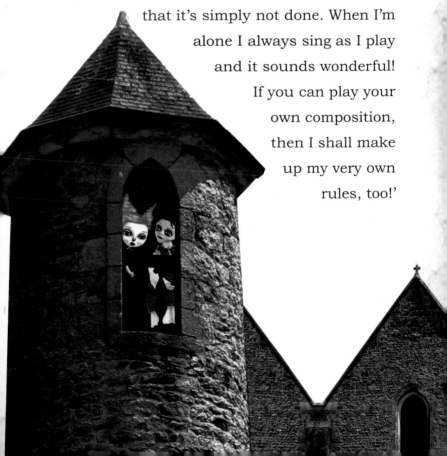

THURSDAY

The first of the month is upon us.

Normal classes were suspended today, and there was an air of anticipation as the students worked to prepare the ballroom. We arranged the fold-out chairs into neat rows, filled vases with fresh flowers from the grounds, and lit the chandeliers carefully. The room glowed warm and golden, and I was filled with thrilling excitement as I took my seat between Albert and Viola, ready to be impressed. The teachers lined up at the back, and it began.

Adeline Miller played her saxophone first – a rich tune with hints of darkness, which put me in mind of special nights with Grandpa Grimstone at home, sharing bitternut chocolates and brandonberry wine in the parlour. Then Albert performed a charming harp solo, which I quietly hummed along to, jiggitying my foot at the same time.

Friederich Ealdwine announced he would perform Piola de Grue's *Vivaci Arduouso Laboriata* and we all gasped, for it's the fastest and most fiddly piece ever composed. Friederich was remarkably loose-fingered, and it was almost perfect, except for a little stumble in the middle that we all forgave him for.

'He'll have the starring role in the benefit concert,' Albert whispered as Friederich received his applause with dignity and aplomb.

When Viola mounted the stage, she ducked her head and sat stiffly at the piano. Her playing was lovely, but I was disappointed. 'What happened to your singing?' I whispered when she'd finished.

'I was too afraid of Mr Bloodworth.'

I put my arm around her. 'Maybe next time you'll be brave enough.' But she shook her head, dejected.

I was scheduled last. I settled onto the Epithium's plush velvet seat, curved my fingers around the strings, and placed my handwritten music sheets on the stand before me. I wasn't even nervous. I just wanted to immerse myself in my music.

As I plucked the first notes of my four-seasons demonstration, the true, honest sounds of the Epithium rang through the ballroom. No longer trying to be a harp, it resonated with rich, heavy notes, gathering my heart and lifting it up, up, until I was soaring.

I summoned the memory of my beloved family – how I long to watch Crumpet orchestrate the fish in the creek; to spy on Grandpa Grimstone in his apothecary…Playing quickly, I pulled frolicking, optimistic notes from the Epithium, and little leaves sprouted from the ornate papered walls of the ballroom. I saw students pointing, gasping, clutching each other. The clouds outside parted, and rays from a pale sun gleamed through the windows. Delicate flowers opened on the wallpaper vines and curtseyed to the audience, who stared around in astonishment. Mr Blanche fainted dead away in the back row.

I deepened my notes next, and the pale rays of the sun became **WARM, HOT, SCORCHING,** until we were all sweating and Madame Sonatine was fanning her face desperately with a clutch of ostrich feathers she'd plucked from her fascinator. Then I quelled the Epithium's strings, subduing my melody, and the heat waned. The wall-leaves darkened, withered, the flowers closed, and the petals and leaves fell to the floor, where they tumbled about.

Stirring my notes, whipping them wilder, I brought in wind – a tiny, fierce whirlwind that swept up the leaves and petals, coiling them into a dramatic spiral before whisking them out through the open double doors. My audience shivered, and I did, too, in the icy-cold mist that filled the room. Exhausted, I played the final notes, and the mist drained away, slithering out the windows and disappearing through tiny cracks in the walls.

Instead of the polite applause we had heard all afternoon, there was silence. Stunned silence. I opened my eyes and glanced around. Mr Bloodworth sat bolt upright in his chair, staring at me with wide bloodshot eyes. Miss Fairclough was reviving Mr Blanche with smelling salts, her sketchbook forgotten at her feet. Madame Sonatine stood motionless, dark tear-streaks down her face where her eye-kohl had run. Suddenly there was a thunderous roar, as the teachers and students all rose to their feet and clapped and cheered.

Remembering my aplomb, I resisted the impulse to run and hide. I pretended to be Lady Sterling herself, bowing my head graciously, stepping from the stage with my back almost as straight as Viola Verlene's. Aunt Gertrude would have been proud. Inside, my heart whirred like a dragonfly's wings.

When the room quieted, Madame Sonatine took the stage. 'Martha Grimstone, I'd no idea you had such skill. My child, you will be famous! You shall feature as the solo in the benefit concert.' She wiped a tear from her cheek.

'At last…the school has a protégée worthy of our distinguished ancestors!'

FRIDAY

My Dearest Diary, things are different.

When I entered the music room this morning, Mr Bloodworth looked at me with interest. Once the first drills were over, he set exercises for the other students and pulled up a stool beside my Epithium.

'This is not a harp, no? What do you call it?' He stroked his beard, polishing it to an even finer point.

'It's an Epithium, sir. My father invented it.'

'The music you played yesterday had the most extraordinary effect upon me – upon us all. I dreamed I saw a whole year pass us by. Do you believe it to be the instrument or the composition that caused this?'

'I'm not sure. I've never played a harp. Only this Epithium. I—'

'Your composition yesterday, was this of your own devising?'

'Yes. Well, mostly. I learned much of it from my father, but I put it all together like that. I've composed some pieces entirely myself, too.' I pulled out my whirlwind inversion composition and held it out. 'I wondered if you might help me with this one? It needs fixing.'

Mr Bloodworth cleared his throat. 'Well, Miss...'

'Miss Grimstone,' I supplied.

'Miss Grimstone, you may spend part of each class furthering your compositions, and I shall give your request some thought. However, you have much to master on a technical front. You must tighten up that somberto. Don't consider this an excuse to drop your focus on trills, chords and pedals.'

'Yes, sir,' I said, keeping my voice subdued, fighting an urge to jump up and down and scream:

'HOORAY!'

FRIDAY

Every day this week Mr Bloodworth has given me time during harp class to work on my own composition. But he never helps me! He is always busy with another student. And I'm stuck.

How, OH HOW, does one permanently inverse a whirlwind?

Instead, I've gone back to my father's last worksheet. I am learning, slowly, to play his piece with the proper pedals. It is incredibly intricate. But something is still not right: when I play it, nothing happens. The clouds don't shift, rain doesn't fall, nor dry up, the wind doesn't change course or stop altogether. And then the piece stops abruptly, unfinished, and that's that.

I stare and stare at all the other squiggles, the squiggles that are not pedal notations nor anything Mr Blanche has shown us, and I know they are telling me something, but WHAT?

It remains a mystery to me.

TUESDAY

The house was quiet tonight – no unveiling of a new invention, nor address by a notable speaker, nor political discourse … no guests. Rose set supper for three in the parlour. She often eats with us when there's no to-do going on, although she never speaks a word.

The parlour was freezing. Lady Sterling, Rose and I huddled under thick blankets and shared a platter of honey-glazed peafowl with puree of pink parsnip. Delicious.

'Are you getting along better at the academy, Martha, now they have seen what you can do?' Lady Sterling asked.

'Yes. I mean, in a fashion. It's just … *when* will Mr Bloodworth assist me with my whirlwind composition? It's been weeks, but the only guidance he gives me concerns the somberto. I need his help!'

'I see your frustration, my dear, but you must remember the school is an old establishment.

Your teachers are highly respected musicians, who'll impart the skills *they* feel you should know. Perhaps you must accomplish their demands of you, before you make demands of them.'

I sighed. 'I'm trying – I really am, Lady Sterling. But sometimes I despair of *ever* being able to meet Mr Bloodworth's demands.'

The doorbell echoed through the house, and a few moments later the butler stepped into the parlour to call for Lady Sterling. It appeared that Misters Chervil and Borage of the Herbaceous Society required her attention this evening after all. She sighed and left, and Rose took this as her cue to clear our plates.

Suddenly alone, I stomped my feet against the cold and decided it was time I gave those bats a firm talking-to.

I pushed my head right up inside the chimney, until I was standing on my very tippy-toes in the hearth.

'Little bats!' I called. 'The chimney sweep is so enamoured of you that he refuses to clean the chimney until you've moved out. Now that's all very well for *you*, but Lady Sterling, Rose and I shall freeze solid if we can't light a fire in this parlour soon. So come down now, my dears, and I will find you a new home for the winter.'

To entice them, I whistled a beautiful little tune, inspired by all the busy sounds I've come to know living in Lady Sterling's manor – the tinkle of her bell in the mornings, the clatter of the kitchen staff preparing supper, and the trundle of carriage wheels on cobblestones...

It worked! One of the baby bats plopped down into my hand. I held out my skirt and it tumbled into it, bouncing with excitement. Then there was a flurry of fur, a beating of wings and a thick cloud of soot as the rest of the extended family tumbled into my dress.

I carried them carefully to my wing and set them on the floor, casting about for something that wouldn't be ruined by all their soot. The only cosy thing I could see was my leather case, so I opened it up and tucked the bats inside, propping the top open with a small pile of books. 'There. It's like a cave, isn't it? I'll find you a proper home tomorrow, I promise.'

But the bats stared back at me uncertainly, and I wasn't sure they liked their new arrangement at all.

WEDNESDAY

This morning every last bat was back in the chimney, and there was a difficult-to-ignore trail of black soot between my wing and the parlour. I was trying to cajole them out again when Lady Sterling called to me, 'Martha, my dear, have you any idea of the time? You're quite late.'

I grabbed my father's final worksheet from beneath my pillow (I keep hoping the answers might come to me in my dreams if I sleep on it enough times), shoved it into my case, and ran the whole way to school – but I still arrived in the music room, breathless, just *after* Mr Bloodworth.

He glared at me. 'You're late! Today we'll play the somberto together as a group, in orchestra form.'

After weeks of practice, I know the trills and chords of Melancholski's somberto with my eyes closed, though I still need to check the annotations on my sheet music to remember which pedal to press when. I opened my case…and saw that my music sheets had been shredded into a bat-shaped nest!

'I…I'm sorry, there's been an unforeseen circumstance,' I stammered. Where was Crumpet when I needed him? He'd have every sheet flattened and each strand lined up in its proper order with a single command.

Mr Bloodworth glared at the mess. 'Careless child! Share Viola's music. I hope *she* has managed to keep her music intact!'

I parked the Epithium next to Viola, who whispered, 'Don't worry about Mr B – he's all pomp and no real fire.'

But when we began, my pedals were wrong. Viola's music was for the piano; there were no annotations. Mr Bloodworth let out a roar of rage.

Faltering, I struck a few more faulty notes on the Epithium before I gave up, closed my eyes and let my fingers do as they would, guided only by the sound of the somberto.

First I just joined the trills, for I knew them well, but once they were over, my fingers spun on, adding little accents here and there – a lilt, a fresh melody above the chords, a little something to push the clouds outside the window away and bring rays of sunshine into the room…By the time the piece finished, sunshine was streaming onto the floor and dust motes shimmered in a floating dance through the air.

Mr Bloodworth crossed his arms, a hint of a smile in his voice. 'Not what I had in mind, Miss Grimstone. And yet there were some nice touches there. I suspect Melancholski would be pleased.'

I ducked my head, forgetting for a moment Madame Sonatine's instructions in aplomb.

'But fetch a fresh somberto score from the front office now, and annotate it again, *promptly*. Go!'

How will I *ever* meet Mr Bloodworth's demands of me? I seem to be thwarted at every turn!

WEDNESDAY

Finally! In my private lesson today, I managed to *talk* to Mr Bloodworth.

'Too much pedal sound. Too much twanging,' he bellowed after I'd played the somberto five times in a row.

I sighed. I am almost there. My trills are good – fast and smooth. And when I re-annotated my score post-bats, I made some adjustments that have improved my pedalwork. Of course, Mr Bloodworth is never satisfied.

I started again, pressing the pedals as delicately as I could, and this time he nodded as I played.

'Better, Miss Grimstone. But you need to practise more. Now, what will you perform for your solo at the benefit concert?'

I held forth my newly written-out whirlwind inversion composition, my plaits prickling with nerves. 'I *want* to play this…only there's something wrong. It uncoils a whirlwind, but not permanently. I can't see how to fix it.'

Mr Bloodworth took the page from me and studied it closely, frowning.

For a very, very long time.

Finally, he spoke.

'Let me be frank with you, Miss Grimstone.' He stroked his beard, pulling it firmly downwards. 'Here at the academy, I groom students for the great stages of the world – to perform in orchestras, as soloists, and with distinguished companies. I have never once groomed a student for storm management. It simply isn't a part of my brief.'

'Perhaps you could do it anyway? I promise not to tell Madame Sonatine!'

'It's not that. I don't mind defying the old girl.' He chuckled heartily. 'I can't help you, though. I simply don't know how.'

I held out my father's last worksheet. 'Have you seen these markings before? My father wrote this.'

'Well, I see this part is a melody. And we have chords, and trills; some harmonics down here. Some pedal annotations…This is an exceptionally challenging piece technically, yes, but it's not impossible. I'm not sure about these symbols here, though. And there seem to be rather a lot of them. Do you know what they mean?'

I shook my head.

'Can you not just ask him?'

'He's dead!'

'Ahh. That poses a problem indeed.' Mr Bloodworth twirled his moustache thoughtfully, and then shook his head. 'But I still can't help you. I'm sorry.'

I stared at Mr Bloodworth in astonishment. All this time I had assumed he was *unwilling* to help me. But in fact, he is unable.

As this
DISASTROUS
news sank in, Dear Diary,
my heart slid
quietly
from
my chest
and slithered
blackly,
weakly,
to the
floor.

SATURDAY

'It's only a few weeks until your concert,' Lady Sterling said. 'Are you looking forward to it?'

I nodded wanly over a forkful of pheasant fricassee. I must say, I eat finely indeed at Lady Sterling's, a refreshing change from the turnip mash with cod-liver oil Aunt Gertrude serves. I can't help but be frightfully homesick, though – especially since my terrible realisation about Mr Bloodworth.

BOOM, BOOM, BOOM, BOOM!

I clapped my hands over my ears and Lady Sterling shot sideways, knocking over the occasional table.

'The only creatures who like that clock are the bats!' she cried. 'Every night they come out to meet it when it chimes. A solution *must* be found, and the chimney sweep is no use – he prefers the wellbeing of those *bats* over our own. Honestly!'

I stared at her, my mouth agape. I'd never seen Lady Sterling lose her temper before.

She cleared her throat. '*Ahem.* Go and dress quickly now, Martha – I have plans for us today. The benefit concert is almost upon us, and you need something gorgeous to wear.'

I realised that although it was a Saturday, Lady Sterling was dressed for the world, her sculpting shirt traded in for an elegant tailored jacket and

lacy skirt. Every hair was curled neatly, drawn high on her head and fastened with ruby-studded pins.

Soon we were in her four-horse coach, clopping grandly into town, and you won't believe where she took me, Dear Diary:

BOBBIN & CO!

Mama will surely faint when I tell her!

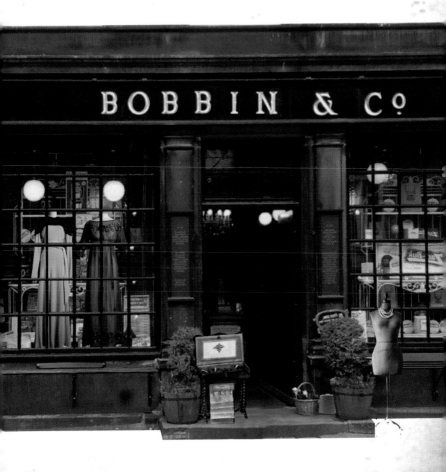

It was an establishment far larger than I'd ever imagined from studying the fabric catalogues with Mama back at home. Its windows spanned TWO ENTIRE BLOCKS, and as we stepped inside I was greeted with familiar scents: fabric dyes, starches, wool and silk. It was like standing in Mama's sewing room. I inhaled deeply.

Lady Sterling led me through the crowds to a small platform surrounded by ornate gold mirrors. She inclined her head graciously, and an attendant hurried over carrying a tape measure. He adjusted his bow tie and cleared his throat. 'At your service, ma'am.'

'We'll need something suitable for a concert hall. She'll be performing,' Lady Sterling announced proudly.

After taking my measurements, the attendant seated us side-by-side on a red velvet sofa and brought us books of fabric samples to study. As I fingered each one, marvelling at the range of colours

and weaves, I wished Mama were with us. How she'd love to choose her fabrics this way, instead of making her best guess from Bobbin & Co's catalogue.

Suddenly Lady Sterling put her arm about my shoulders. 'Martha, my dear, whatever is the matter? You've been downcast for days.'

I started, for I'd done my best to remain cheerful lest Lady Sterling think me ungrateful.

'Is it about the concert? It is a great honour to play the closing solo at the academy's famous benefit concert, you know.'

'I…you…it's not that I'm not thrilled, Lady Sterling,' I sputtered. 'It's just…I don't see *magic* anywhere at the school,' I confessed in a rush. 'Not in any spots at all. I thought my teachers would show me how to harness it.'

'Oh, Martha, there *is* magic at the school. It's within *you*, my dear.'

'But…I need magic from outside of me! I need to be taught how to use it. That's why I came.'

Lady Sterling shook her head. 'When I invited you here, I thought the school would help with your technique. Has it not?'

I nodded. 'I am improving, yes. But what's the point of flawless arpeggios, trills and pedal-work if I can't use them to work magic in the sky?'

'You *will*, Martha. You must take whatever you can learn here and use it in your own magical way, even if that's not as your teachers expect. Each technique you learn now will help you someday, somehow, to find what you are looking for. I'm sure of it.'

A tear trickled down my cheek. I managed a grateful smile.

'Now, perhaps this one?' Lady Sterling suggested, bringing my attention back to the samples on our laps – and I gasped, for such a fabric would be breathtakingly expensive. It was a cool blue, so soft it slipped between my fingers, finer than silk, but warmer and somehow richer. It made me think of Miss Fairclough's sailor dress, though that is made of an ordinary linen.

Lady Sterling signalled for the attendant, who bounded back to us in an instant. 'Now to select a style,' he recommended, clearly pleased with Lady Sterling's choice.

We were shown illustrations of girls wearing

dresses of all possible designs – some with wide crinolines, others narrow with a wasp waist; some with heavy bustles, others with lace shawls. But I couldn't stop thinking of Miss Fairclough's dress, and in the end I pulled out my pencil and a slip of paper and drew for the attendant what I wanted. I made the skirt longer, more appropriate to a performance that would require aplomb and grace, and added a red ribbon at the neck.

red ribbon at neck

He took my drawing and said to Lady Sterling, 'Your daughter is very talented.'

I flushed, as much at the idea of Lady Sterling being my mama as at his compliment. Before Lady Sterling could correct him, he'd moved to a glass-topped bench to jot down the numbers and measurements. When I heard the price I was horrified, but Lady Sterling calmly handed him several notes.

'Thank you,' I whispered as we threaded through the crowd towards the exit.

'Nothing is too much for my *daughter*.' Lady Sterling winked at me, and we both giggled – but then I thought again of my real mama, and how she would have loved to be there with me.

MONDAY

Tonight, as I sat in bed sipping my milk, I was flipping through the pages of my whirlwind and meteorological compositions, trying to remember where the emotions go, when…

I HAD AN IDEA!

If I can annotate piano music to translate it into harp music – to show the harpist where to pedal – then why couldn't I do just such a thing to remind me where to put the *emotion* into my own music? To translate regular music into magical music…

And I did it, Dear Diary! I created a lilting symbol for my joy, and a terrible slash for my deepest anger…a tentative little sign for first hope, a bold one for outrage…And so it went, until I'd created my very own alphabet – Martha's Magnificent Menagerie of Emotions!

ϕ = first hope

π = joy

IO = contentment

λ = wistfulness

$\mathcal{f}$ = restlessness

$\boxminus$ = moroseness

Λ = anger

$\boxtimes$ = outrage

I immediately set to work adding these annotations to my whirlwind worksheets, in a wild flurry of inspiration. *Oh! Oh! Oh!* And somewhere in the midst of that swirling tempest of my happiness and rage and passion – so caught up in it I wasn't *thinking* about anything else, except perhaps that it would've made things far easier if my *father* had done this, too, since after decoding his first piece I was still left to figure out all by myself that I could only bring rain if I introduced certain emotions at certain points in the music –

I HAD IT!

I leapt out of bed with a circus-lady flip so high that I swung right over the dancing fish above me. Oops! I leapt back again, and snatched my father's last worksheet from beneath my pillow.

YES!!! The final worksheet. The one I cannot fully decipher. All its odd little symbols … suddenly they didn't look so different to my very own squiggles! Different shapes to mine, true. Different sizes, different line weights…but now, Dear Diary, I am sure, absolutely SURE, that I know what they are:

The last set of mysterious markings I've never understood are the code to my father's emotions! His final, incomplete composition, written on the very day of his death, dictates EXACTLY which emotions are needed to harness its power — and there are a lot of them!

No wonder I've not been able to understand it. Music is written to a standard code, always using the same symbols, so that anyone can play a piece. But emotions? Each person is different, individual. There is no standard code for another's emotions.

To understand Mortimer's final song, perhaps I need to find a way to truly understand my father himself…

I lay awake all night, my eyes wide open, my thoughts a whirlwind inside my head.

This is brilliant! Simply

BRILLIANT!

(Or, if I use my Magnificent Menagerie of Emotions: 不)

Now that dawn has risen, however, and I've finally grown weary, I ache for my family. I know I must be strong, Dear Diary, but I do wish I could discuss with them all that I've discovered.

SATURDAY

This morning I got up early, crept to the parlour and greeted the bats … for I had a plan.

The mama bat flew down onto my arm at once, but all the babies remained ensconced in the chimney. Softly I hummed to them, a sweet tune Viola Verlene taught me. I tapped my bare feet against the hearth in rhythm.

A tiny baby bat dropped into my palm. I carefully placed it on my arm next to the mama, its tail curling around me to hold on tight. Then another baby bat dropped, and another, and at last a beating of furry wings and flashing of tails brought the entire family into the fireplace. I scooped them into my skirt.

'Come on. It's been a long winter without the fire. But I've a new idea for you – a home I think you'll like far more than my case.'

I opened the door of the grandfather clock and gently tipped the bats onto its floor. They stared around in bewilderment, but I was ready for them this time. I'd collected branches from the vamprenoc

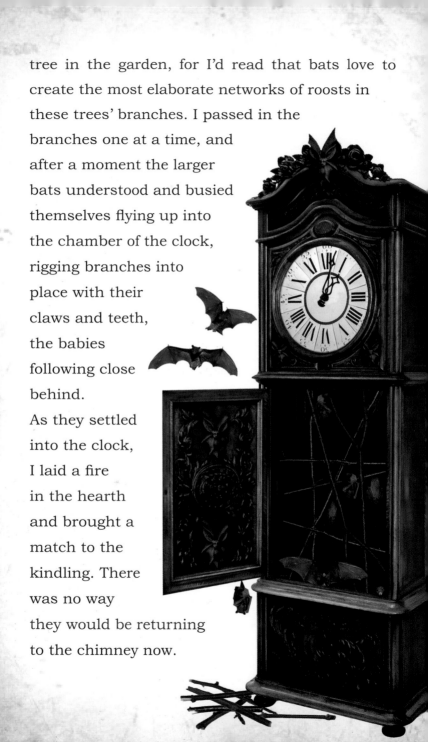

tree in the garden, for I'd read that bats love to create the most elaborate networks of roosts in these trees' branches. I passed in the branches one at a time, and after a moment the larger bats understood and busied themselves flying up into the chamber of the clock, rigging branches into place with their claws and teeth, the babies following close behind.

As they settled into the clock, I laid a fire in the hearth and brought a match to the kindling. There was no way they would be returning to the chimney now.

By the time Lady Sterling emerged from her workshop, flames were crackling and the room glowed with heat for the first time in months.

'Oh, Martha!' she cried, flinging her arms around me. 'How I love having you here. Now come quickly, for I have something to show *you*, too!' And she rushed me to her workshop, where she gestured with a flourish towards her sculpture, finished at last.

'I think that's her. Tempesta. What do you think?'

'She's magnificent,' I replied reverently.

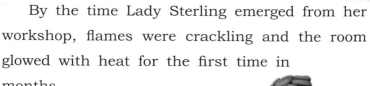

FRIDAY

Today, the day of the benefit concert, was so windy at first that I actually blew part of the way from Lady Sterling's manor to the Queen's Music Academy.

The day was filled with frantic back-to-back rehearsals in the ballroom. Mr Bloodworth had us run through the somberto again and again, shouting at us intermittently and pacing the room, turning his beard into a wild mess. Viola was trembling with nerves, and poor Albert looked frightfully pale. Me, I couldn't help but feel a ripple of excitement...

Meanwhile, the ballroom was brought to life as flurries of staff came and went with ladders and mops. Instead of the rows of metal chairs, a seating bank was hired, every seat plush with velvet. Behind that, the room was filled with tables laden with bubbling champagne and delicate hors d'oeuvres.

AT LAST, the doors were thrown open to welcome our guests. We students were hidden in the orchestra pit, and we huddled together nervously as Madame Sonatine greeted a seemingly never-ending stream of people we'd read about in books and newspapers, or seen framed in the portraits in the academy's hallways. I knew Lady Sterling would be out there somewhere, and pride billowed in my heart to know she was here to see *me*.

Mr Bloodworth, now freshly polished and pointed, was doing his best to convince everyone that the Queen's Music Academy was the most superior institution in the land. Suddenly he loomed above us, peering into the gloom of the pit, and clapped his hands: our cue to begin.

We filed onto the stage – each student of the school, one by one, standing as tall as we could. As instructed by Madame Sonatine, we graciously inclined our heads to the audience as we made our way to our instruments. I looked into the sea of expectant faces, but I couldn't see Lady Sterling.

The orchestra piece went well, and I marvelled at how much I'd learned in under a year. I trilled quickly and competently, my pedals were almost silent, and my chords were resonant and lovely. In fact, everybody played brilliantly. The applause from the audience was enthusiastic as we bowed, the lights dazzling our eyes, and within moments we were filing off the stage so that the advanced students could play their solos.

Friederich Ealdwine's performance was dashing, a breakneck whirl of blistering notes, and there was much murmuring amongst the crowd as he left the stage.

Albert's piece was marvellous until he elbowed his music stand, toppling it right over, and had to be rescued by Mr Bloodworth, who hurried onto the stage and held out the sheets by hand. Poor Albert was so flustered that his piece didn't quite come together after that, which was a terrible shame.

'Sing! You can do it!' I whispered loudly to Viola when it was her turn.

'Remember, Mr B is all pomp but no real fire. Don't be afraid.'

Viola hesitated for an awkward moment at the piano, and I held my breath. She raised her fingers and struck the first notes, playing as usual...but a few bars in, I heard something lovely as a bird, lulling and beautiful.

Viola was singing!

Softly at first, but increasing in volume, she created another whole melody right on top of the one she was playing, the notes crisscrossing delightfully, complex and enchanting. When she'd finished, Albert and I clapped so hard that Lady Sonatine was forced to ask for silence.

And then it was my turn.

I gave Viola a quick squeeze as we passed on the stairs. Her face was flushed, her eyes shining. Onstage, the lights felt brighter, hotter than before. I dropped a polite curtsey and seated myself at the Epithium. Outside, the wind howled against the ballroom windows; the panes rattled and the chandeliers flickered. Before me, on the music stand, stood my whirlwind inversion composition. It didn't matter that it wouldn't quash a whirlwind permanently. It was still a dramatic, enticing melody, and I'd composed it entirely myself.

As I brought my fingers to the strings, a small sound from the audience caught my ear...

The word floated in the air for a few suspended seconds before I raised my eyes slowly to the most *magnificent* sight:

my family, sitting in a row in the audience beside Lady Sterling. I gasped.

Mama was leaning forward, her cheeks rosy and her eyes bright with expectation. Grandpa Grimstone sat upright, a proud smile across his face. Crumpet was whispering something else – I could see his lips moving, his hands motioning – and Aunt Gertrude was shushing him. August, his hand on Aunt Gertrude's shoulder, sent me a warm, encouraging smile. *You can do this, Miss Martha*, I could see him thinking. Then Crumpet let loose with a fistful of *sparks*, my heart soared with joy, and the music began.

I kept my gaze firmly on my family, so thrilled to see them at last, and I played for them. Every note held a message: *How I've missed you! At last you're here!* I didn't need to look at my sheet music; I knew it well, and played it faithfully.

My new skills took over as my music took flight – trills faster even than the somberto's; delightful lilting sounds that caught at the heart-strings - and suddenly my melody was transformed. Instead of following what I'd written, I diverged. As I hit the high notes, my fingers moved into new trills – fast, brilliant bursts I'd never played before. Not the trills of the somberto, exactly; trills that belonged only to the Epithium, my fingers made deft, accurate, by the many months of practice.

I knew we hadn't a whirlwind nearby, but the wind outside began to flatten, the howling against the windows quietening to a low rattle. I smiled, knowing that if my music was commanding the weather, it would be touching the hearts of the audience, too. And so we rode the melody together, filled as it was with sweetness and tears and sadness, inspired by my longing and love for my family, but carrying each of us to our own personal magical place. For Mama, it was as if she were with Mortimer. Me, I was cradled with my family. For Lady Sterling and Madame Sonatine…who knew?

As my music drew to a close, the audience stood and cheered, throwing their corsages and their hats while I, with aplomb, curtseyed and left the spotlight. Miss Fairclough dabbed Madame Sonatine's face and refreshed the kohl beneath her eyes before allowing her to mount the stage.

'There are no words that can follow the accomplishment of my students,' she began. But the words did follow, and Madame Sonatine outlined for the audience the tears and sweat we'd wrought as we struggled to prepare for this day. 'They are the hardest-working, most prodigious pupils. I present to you… the new aristocracy of the music world!'

Back in the orchestra pit, Viola Verlene stifled a giggle and Albert rolled his eyes. 'If only she really thought that about us,' he managed to whisper before Mr Bloodworth silenced him with a gesture.

'AND NOW,' Madame Sonatine went on, 'I would like to announce the prize for the most improved student, a mere first-year, who has many years ahead of her at this school in which to further her skill: Martha Grimstone!'

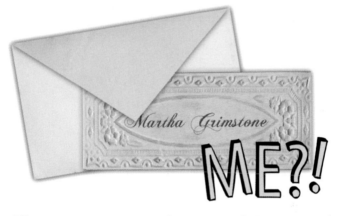

There was more applause, and I was pushed back onto the stage, where I took my place beside Madame Sonatine. My whole family stood, faces pink with pleasure, clapping vigorously.

'You may speak,' Madame Sonatine said as the applause died down.

I'd had no idea I was to give a speech. I stood flummoxed, my mouth opening and closing like one of the fish on my bed back at Lady Sterling's.

I forced myself to focus on the crowd before me. 'I…Thank you! I'm so glad I came here!' And I was, despite my misgivings. 'I've learned more technical skills than I ever thought I could.' I glanced at Mr Bloodworth. 'And I've loved discovering art as well as music.' I slid my eyes from Miss Fairclough to Lady Sterling.

Outside, the wind remained silent. Maybe this new version of my composition *will* permanently destroy a whirlwind!

At that thought, Dear Diary, I took a very, *very* deep breath…

'I adore you, Lady Sterling.' I found her again in the audience and saw her cheeks were pink with pleasure. 'I love our messy, quiet Saturdays; the way you listen to me and encourage me. I love the grandeur of your house, the statues and arbours of your garden, and my glorious guest wing.

'Albert, I love your cheeky whispers – and Viola, your beautiful, lilting voice, and your wonderful friendship. But I am a guest in this city, and right now all I want is to go home! I want to be back in my own valley of magic, where I can bring rain with my Epithium and people will celebrate that. And I simply MUST test out my whirlwind composition now!' There were some confused faces in the audience, but I could see August nodding approvingly.

I turned to Madame Sonatine. 'I'm sorry,' I said shakily, 'for I won't be return-ing to the school next term.'

There was a collective gasp from the audience, and Madame Sonatine's gracious smile turned frosty.

I thought briefly again of my wing at Lady Sterling's house – of all I was giving up. Was I mad? And yet I knew my decision was the right one.

'I've work to do at home,' I pressed on. 'My valley needs me, and I shall use the skills I have learned here to find a way to save it.'

August sprung to his feet and cheered loudly, hammering his hands together in delight. Crumpet emitted an entire cloud of sparkling coloured bubbles, which floated delicately amongst the chandeliers. Grandpa Grimstone stood; then so did Mama, Lady Sterling and Aunt Gertrude. And suddenly the entire room was alive, celebrating my plans for the following year. Even Madame Sonatine, seeing the audience's delight, couldn't help but smile and bow, as though this had been her own doing.

I kissed the air beside Madame Sonatine's cheek, and then it was over, and we students were released into the audience to find our people.

'Mama! Grandpa Grimstone! Here!' I cried, and they pushed through the crowd towards me. But just as I was about to hurl myself upon them, somebody took my hand.

'Martha? My parents would like to meet you,' Viola said, and I turned to find her standing between a stout man and a tall, wiry woman.

Viola passed my hand to her father, who bowed forward and kissed it, much to my astonishment, for I don't think my hand has ever been kissed before.

Viola's mother took hold of me by both shoulders. 'Child! Where did you learn to play like that? I know it couldn't have been here...'

Before I could answer, she continued: 'And I

always thought *singing* while onstage would be vulgar for a true musician, but the audience tonight showed how much they loved Viola's voice. I hear you've encouraged her. Bravo! We'll be taking her to perform with us in Wailingham. She'll sing, and we'll employ a pianist. We've an engagement with the Royal Family, an event requiring us to be at our finest yet. Well, our finest since…since…'

I knew then that she was thinking of Viola's brother, but before I could offer my condolences she went on, fast and breathless: 'In any case, we thought perhaps you'd like to join us, just for this booking? While we search for a pianist. Think of the reaction, if you and Viola were to perform together…We could replace Viola's piano work with your…your…*instrument*. And then we'll introduce the—'

Viola's father laid his hand on her arm. 'Let the girl breathe, dear. Her family is waiting to say hello. Don't worry, I won't let anyone else snap her up.' And to me, he added: 'We'd pay you handsomely, of course.'

Crumpet launched himself into my arms and fastened himself around my neck. I laughed and kissed his face a hundred times, breathing his familiar smell of boilberry tea.

Mama wrapped her arms around both of us, and held me so tightly I couldn't breathe. I pressed my cheek against hers.

'Oh, Martha! We've missed you so!'

Grandpa Grimstone, Aunt Gertrude and August each took their turn to squeeze their arms between Mama's and Crumpet's, embracing me. Lady Sterling took me by the shoulders, kissed my forehead, and said, 'Martha, you have outdone yourself! I am so proud of you.'

Grandpa Grimstone shook hands with Viola's father, while Aunt Gertrude complimented Viola on both her playing and her incredible poise. To Lady Sterling, I said, 'I'm sorry, I'm ever so grateful to you for having me. I just can't stay…'

But Lady Sterling wrapped her arm around me and said, 'You have what you came for, my dear. Now go home and make use of your new skills.'

Viola leaned through everyone to whisper, 'If you say yes to my parents, they'll leave you in peace. *Do* say yes! We'll have such fun! Just imagine!'

So I wriggled out of Mama's grasp and, still holding Crumpet firmly to my hip, I said to Mr and Mrs Verlene, 'Thank you, I should be delighted to accept your invitation.'

Then Aunt Gertrude took out a notepad and demanded all the details, and I swelled with pleasure, for I knew how much a handsome sum would help towards the many repairs needed at home. I turned back to Viola, to introduce her to my family. Outside, the wind remained silent.

My Dearest Diary, magnificence is blooming indeed! I *have* learned some of what I needed to know here, after all. Well, I cannot be sure until I've tested my inversion composition on a real whirlwind. Or proven that the squiggles on my father's final worksheet *are* emotions. But I understand now that I came here to master trills, harmonics and arpeggios, and to learn how to write down my compositions, including the parts that give them their power.

These are the tools I shall use to harness the magic that turns back a storm. I shall inverse a whirlwind, I shall translate my father's final piece, or, if need be, I shall find another way altogether. Lady Sterling is right – it's up to me now, to work out how to do this, and I feel strangely confident that I *can* do it. In the meantime, perhaps I will find another tool, another piece of the answer, in Wailingham…or at the very least, as the lovely Viola says, have such fun as I can only imagine.

The Making of the Grimstones

Dear Reader,

I made the family of Grimstone puppets myself, and furnished their miniature home. This was for my gothic theatre show, *The Grimstones*. It took me eighteen months to handcraft everything, mostly from recycled junk. They were some of the happiest days of my life, because nothing gives me more pleasure than making things with my own hands.

Since my partner, Paula Dowse, and I began performing with the Grimstones, as puppeteers and narrators for the show, we have toured Australia and the world. It seems that, like me, our audiences have fallen in love with my little puppet family.

Between shows, Martha Grimstone sits on her tiny bed and scrawls in her notebook, unleashing all the excitements and frustrations of her everyday life. Her

words are captivating, her little drawings so enchanting, that I can't help myself from sharing them with you. Every time I take one of her notebooks I leave an empty one in its place, and she winks at me, because Martha longs to be famous and can't wait for you to read her diary!

If you would like to know more about the Grimstones, please visit **www.thegrimstones.com**. You can watch them come to life on YouTube, download beautiful photos of their miniature world, and see where they'll be performing next. Find the Grimstones on Facebook, follow them on Twitter, and read my blog.

Online, you can also order *The Grimstones – An Artist's Journal*, which records my creative process while making the Grimstones puppets and show, from my initial spark of an idea through to a theatrical production that has toured the world. It's jam-packed with sketches, beautiful photographs and 'how to' tips, providing inspiration to create and bring more creativity into your life.

Thank you for sharing the Grimstones with me.

Love and creative fire to you!

THE GRIMSTONES

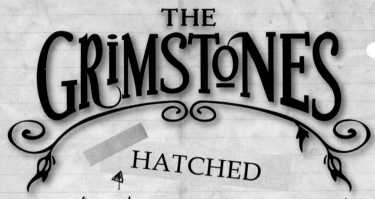

HATCHED

My first diary—lots of secrets inside!
All about Crumpet !!

MORTIMER REVEALED

My second diary—
discover the secrets
of Mortimer's
crypt!

WHIRLWIND

My third diary—in which
there are rabbits!

Make sure you read
the first three books
in The Grimstones
series.